About this Book

This story is about Lucy and Tom Cat. They are on their way to the beach where their amazing adventure begins.

LUCY

·Tom Cat·

Keep your eyes open for clues. If you get stuck there are answers on pages 31 and 32.

Turn the page for a great adventure.

On the Beach

Lucy sat on a rock on the beach, reading a fantastic adventure story about dragons and monsters. Tom Cat was nearby watching fish jump.

Waves lapped against Lucy's rock and crashed onto the shore. Her tummy rumbled. It was nearly supper time.

Tom Cat yowled as a wave washed over him. Lucy looked up. She couldn't see anything. But there was something that Lucy had not spotted. It was in the water, coming closer and closer.

Look at the opposite page. Can you see what it is?

4

Lucy Meets the Sea Monster

Lucy turned around and gulped as the monster reared up out of the waves. She had never seen anything like it before, except in her book. It was green, with a long snaky body, knobbly skin and wobbly antennae on its head. It had spikes like a dragon along its back, but it looked friendly.

Imagine Lucy's surprise when the strange creature began to speak.

"Hello," it said. "My name's Horace. I'm a sea monster."

"H...h...hello," stammered Lucy. "I'm Lucy and this is Tom Cat." But where WAS Tom Cat? He had vanished.

Can you spot Tom Cat?

The Adventure Begins

"I must rescue Tom Cat!" Lucy exclaimed.

"I'll help you," said Horace. "Climb onto my back."

Lucy looked doubtfully at Horace's spikes, but when she touched one it was surprisingly soft. She jumped up and held on tightly. Horace's tail snaked from side to side and they whizzed away, whooshing through the waves.

A sleek silvery shape suddenly leapt up and dived quickly down again, but not before Lucy caught sight of a beady eye and cheeky, friendly grin.

Dolphins!
There were lots of
them, on all sides,
chattering and dancing around
Horace and Lucy.

"Have you seen my cat?" Lucy asked them.

"Try Blue Bird Island," one called, pushing a map
of the islands into Lucy's hand.

Which one do you think is Blue Bird Island?

Blue Bird Island

"We're here," Horace said, cheerily.

Lucy jumped ashore on Blue Bird Island and heard the sounds of splashing and shouting nearby. She raced along the rocky beach and found some children tying up their boat. Lucy was aware of eyes watching in the distance, behind the trees.

I saw a cat about to land on One Tree Island.

10

There was no sign of Tom Cat here, but one of the children had seen him and the others gave her helpful directions. She had to find One Tree Island. Lucy stared at the islands across the bay.

Can you find One Tree Island?

The island has a tower on it ...

... with a pointed turret, like a witch's hat ...

... and no other buildings.

Finn the Fishergirl

Horace zipped across to One Tree Island where they met a little fishergirl. She began to speak to them, but what she said was in rhyme.

"Finn is my name
and if you'll help with my game,
I'll put you on track
to get your cat back."

It was very puzzling, but slowly Lucy and Horace began to understand Finn. They agreed to help her with her game and in return, she told them what they must do to follow Tom Cat.

"Through a maze made of coral, that's the first thing to do.
The route through is tricky, but here is a clue:
look out for clear water, beware the sharp rocks,
watch out for the sharks and avoid any shocks.

12

Next stop is Shell Isle and there you must find
twelve shells shaped like starfish – the bright yellow kind.
Give these to old Toby, and he will quite soon
show you the way to the great Lost Lagoon.
And now for my game that you promised to play,
I can't play alone, I've been trying all day.
You must use your eyes and do as I bid –
find how many squids you can see here with Sid."

A little squid wiggled a wavy
tentacle at Lucy. It was Sid, but
he was the only squid she could
see. Or was he?

**Can you find Sid? How
many other squids
can you see?**

The Coral Maze

Horace and Lucy said goodbye and set off for the coral maze.

"It's not going to be easy to find a way through," Horace said when they arrived. "The coral is spiky and sharp and there are dangers lurking."

The white flag marks the way out to the open sea. Can you find a way through the maze, steering clear of the spiky coral and lurking creatures?

Shell Isle

"Phew, I'm glad that's over," said Horace, when they reached the end of the coral maze. "Now let's go to Shell Isle to search for the shells for Toby."

Lucy gasped with astonishment when she saw Shell Isle. Everywhere she looked there were shells gleaming and glittering in the sunshine. There was a shell jetty, a hut made from shells and even a shell boat. The shells looked so pretty that Lucy began to collect them in a basket.

Then she remembered that she had to find some special shells.

Lucy darted up and down. She soon found the twelve yellow star shaped shells and they were ready to look for Toby at the gateway to the Lost Lagoon.

Can you spot the twelve yellow star shells that Lucy needs?

The Lost Lagoon

When Lucy saw Toby she was speechless. He had a fishy tail!

"You're a merman!" she spluttered.

Toby smiled down at her over his glasses. He swished his scaly tail and counted his shells.

"You can go into the Lagoon now," he said.

They sailed on into the Lost Lagoon. At the far side, there were amazing tutti frutti trees growing along the banks.

Just as Lucy and Horace were wondering what to do next, a face popped out of the leaves.

"Hello! I'm Olivia, I study birds," she called. "I get a bird's eye view of the island from up here. I can help you find your furry friend — if you will help me first. I'm trying to find the Golden Spotted Wonderbird. Its tail has five gold spotted feathers which curl up at the ends. If you can spot it for me, I'll tell you which way your cat went."

Can you spot the Golden Spotted Wonderbird?

The Rainbow River

When Olivia saw the Wonderbird she almost fell out of her tree with excitement.

"Your cat went that way, along the Rainbow River," she pointed.

Lucy stared at the winding, whirling waterway. "It looks a bit choppy," she said.

Horace began to swim. Waves whipped up as the river rushed and swirled, hurrying them onward until... Oh no! SPLASH! SPLUTTER!

Lucy and Horace dived over the edge of a waterfall. Coughing and gasping they bobbed up to the surface again. The Rainbow River roared and raced along to the sea. Suddenly Lucy caught sight of something very familiar.

What has Lucy spotted?

Under the Sea

Tom Cat whizzed around and around in a whirlpool, spinning and sinking down below the waves.

"There's only one way for you to follow him," said Horace, "And luckily help is at hand."

To Lucy's surprise, a small fish began gulping air. With each gulp, the fish puffed up and grew bigger and bigger, until it was enormous.

"It's a puffa fish," Horace told Lucy. "Sit very still."

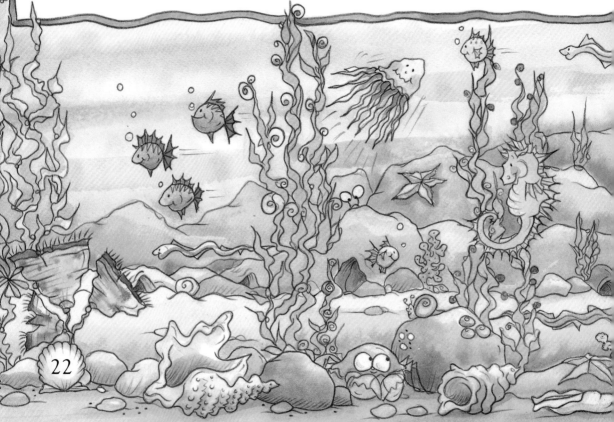

With that, the fish blew a giant air bubble around Lucy. Horace dived under the water with her. Down and down he swam, through the depths of the sea.

From inside her bubble, Lucy watched the wonderful, underwater world. At the bottom, a strange fish began talking. It spoke each word in a bubble, but the words were all jumbled.

What is the fish's message?

MONSTERS'

CASTLE

THE

GO

SEA

TO

The Galleon

Lucy watched shimmering fish flash past. Two turtles chased each other through coral arches and waving weeds. The reeds rippled apart and Lucy stared ahead into the black mouth of a dark cave and tunnel.

Horace disappeared inside and Lucy followed. The
tunnel ended and Lucy blinked in surprise.
A splendid sunken galleon lay half-buried in the sand.
But Lucy couldn't see Horace anywhere.

Where is Horace? Can you find him?

25

Horace's Home

"Hold tight," said Horace. "I have a surprise for you."

Lucy clung on to Horace's tail until suddenly she lost her grip. She bounced down and down, tumbling bumpety, bumpety, BUMP. She landed on soft sand and sat staring up at a fantastic fairytale castle.

"It's my home," said Horace. "And here are my family and friends. They all want to meet you but they're a bit shy."

Family? Friends? Lucy could only see fish and funny fishy monsters. But Horace explained that the sea monsters were the ones with two wobbly antennae on their heads.

How many sea monsters do you think there are?

Surprise Party

Lucy followed Horace inside the castle. Her bubble popped and she found she could breathe without it. Horace introduced her to all sorts of sea creatures and led her on to a tall, arched doorway. The gleaming shell doors slowly opened.

Lucy gazed at a sea of faces. The monsters and their friends were sitting at a long table in the longest room Lucy had ever seen. They all began to speak at once.

"We're having a party to celebrate your visit," said Nessie, Horace's sister. "Our other special guest is already here."

Who is the other special guest?

Goodbye

Lucy gave Tom Cat a big hug and squeeze before she was whisked away to dance. The wonderful party passed in a whirl. Lucy ate and sang and danced . . . until suddenly it was time to go.

Lucy and Tom Cat climbed onto Horace's back and waved goodbye to their new friends. Almost before they knew it, they were back at the beach where their adventure had begun.

"I don't want to say goodbye to you, Horace," Lucy said, hugging him.

Horace smiled, "But I'll see you again very soon."

Lucy and Tom Cat jumped down onto the sandy shore and waved to Horace as he swam back to sea.

"Lucy!" called the familiar voice of her mother. "It's time for supper!"

Answers

Pages 4-5

A green sea monster is coming closer and closer to Lucy's rock. It is ringed in the picture.

Pages 6-7

Tom Cat is being washed out to sea.

Pages 8-9

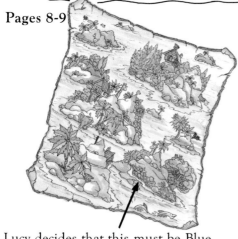

Lucy decides that this must be Blue Bird Island. It is the only one with blue birds on it.

Pages 10-11

This is One Tree Island. It has only one tree, a tower with a pointed turret and there are no other buildings on it.

Pages 12-13

There are 11 little squids including Sid. You can see them all ringed here in the picture.

This is Sid the Squid.

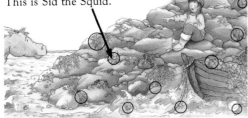

Pages 14-15

Lucy's and Horace's way through the coral maze to the open sea is marked in red.

Pages 16-17
You can see the twelve yellow stars that Lucy has to find ringed here.

Pages 18-19
This is the Golden Spotted Wonderbird. Can you see his five curly tail feathers?

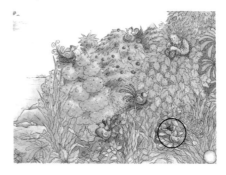

Pages 20-21
Lucy has spotted Tom Cat. Here he is.

Pages 22-23
When you put all the words in the right order, the fish's message is, "GO TO THE SEA MONSTER'S CASTLE."

Pages 24-25
Here is Horace. He is well hidden behind the plants.

Pages 26-27
You can see the ten sea monsters marked here.

Pages 28-29
Did you spot the other special guest? It is Tom Cat.

CHOCOLATE ISLAND

Karen Dolby

Illustrated by Caroline Church

Contents

About this Story

This story is about Tom and Grace and their amazing adventures on Chocolate Island. It all begins one day when they spot a poster for a chocolate cake baking competition . . .

Chunkies Chocolate Cakes and Cookies Competition

to bake the Best Ever Chocolate Cake

Sensational Prizes:
World fame as a cook. Television appearances. Lifetime's supply of chocolate cakes and cookies

Turn the page for a great adventure.

Keep your eyes open for clues. If you get stuck there are answers on pages 63 and 64.

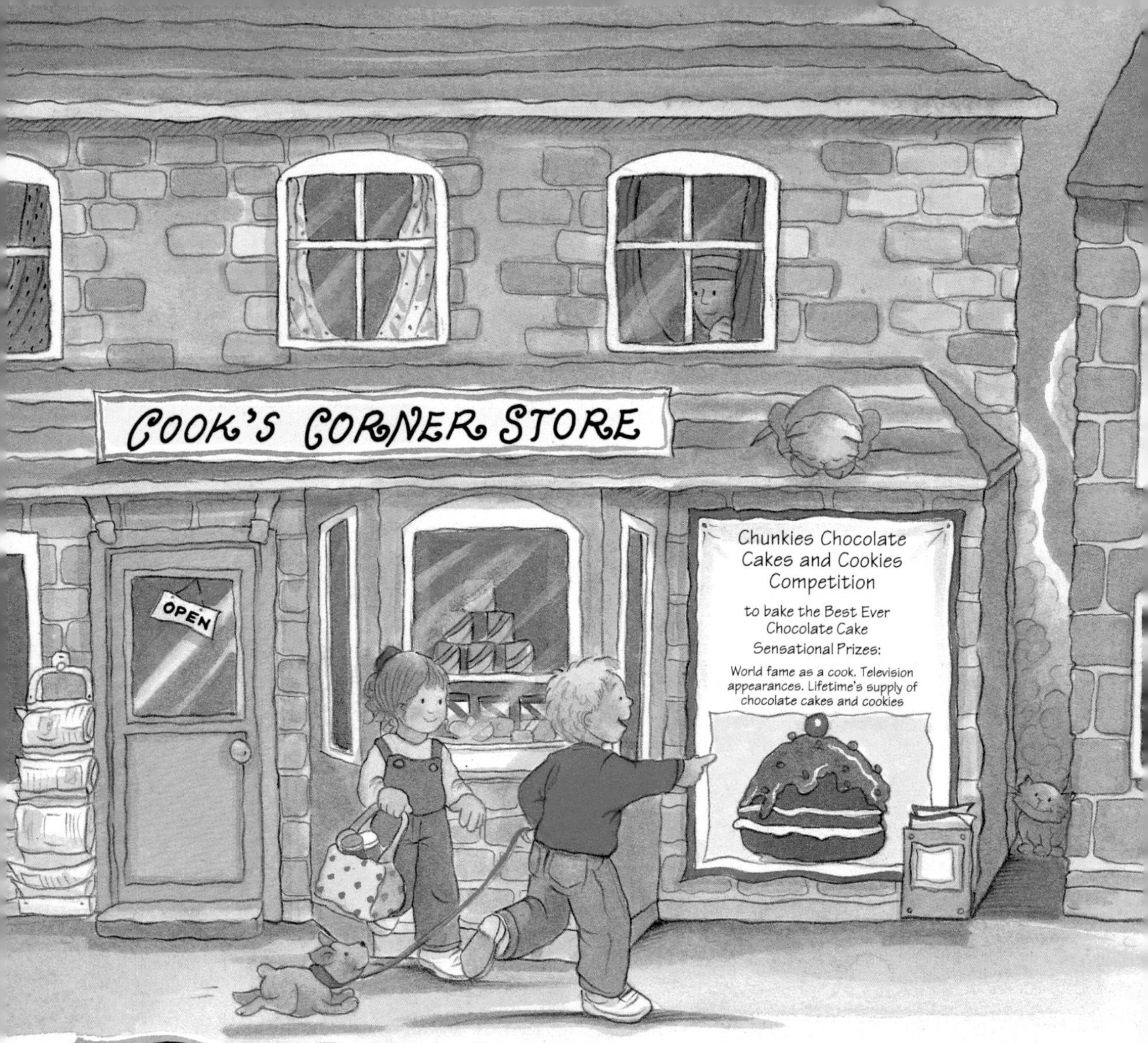
COOK'S CORNER STORE
OPEN
Chunkies Chocolate
Cakes and Cookies
Competition
to bake the Best Ever
Chocolate Cake
Sensational Prizes:
World fame as a cook. Television
appearances. Lifetime's supply of
chocolate cakes and cookies

Chocolate Cake Baking Competition

When Tom and Grace saw the Chunkies Cake Baking Competition poster they were very excited. Their Great Uncle Ollie baked the yummiest chocolate cakes and they were sure he could win the prize.

"Think of all the chocolate we could win," said Grace.

"And we could appear on TV with Uncle Ollie – we'd be famous," added Tom.

They raced to Uncle Ollie's house. "We want you to make a chocolate cake – your best ever," exclaimed Tom, waving the competition leaflet at his Uncle.

"I'm afraid I can't see a thing without my spectacles," Ollie said. "And I seem to have lost them. I was sorting out this old chest when I last saw them."

Can you spot Uncle Ollie's spectacles?

Granny Truffle's Story

Uncle Ollie sighed. "I've no chance with Mrs. Nougat around. She always wins competitions and her chocolate cake is famous."

Tom and Grace shuddered. "Mrs. Nougat – yuck! She's horrible and everyone says she cheats."

Uncle Ollie sighed. "My Granny Truffle made THE best chocolate cake. Now, if I had her recipe and some Chocolate Island chocolate, then my cake would be a winner. My Granny used to tell me stories about a fantastic island with a chocolate well, chocolate drop trees, and chocolate fudge streams."

"Just imagine the most deliciously yummy chocolate anyone has ever tasted, bubbling up from the ground. I used to have dreams about the island, wishing and wishing I could go there. A long time ago now . . ."

"And did you ever go there?" asked Tom.

"Oh no," smiled Ollie, mysteriously. "Although Granny did draw me a map showing where the island is. It's here somewhere. It's easy to spot because it has the Chocolate Island symbol of a moon and star in the corner."

Can you see the Chocolate Island map?

The Old Map

Grace and Tom lifted out the old map.
As they looked at it, they decided they
MUST visit Chocolate Island.

Ollie's House

Chocolate
Island
Ferry

If Uncle Ollie was going to bake the winning chocolate cake and beat ghastly Mrs. Nougat, it was up to them to find the special Chocolate Island chocolate for him. **Which do you think is Chocolate Island? (Look for its sign.)**

Aboard the Chocolate Queen

They dashed down to the seashore where a strange old boat was bobbing up and down in the waves, ready to set sail. Captain Cook welcomed them aboard.

"Hold tight for the journey of a lifetime," she laughed. And they were off. Wizzz! Wooosh! Wooo!

It felt as if they were flying. But they zoomed along at such a pace it was hard to tell. The boat slowed.

"Chocolate Island ahoy!" their Captain shouted.

Tom leaned over the side, eager to catch his first glimpse of Chocolate Island. But which one was it? Soon Tom spotted a chocolate fudge stream, chocolate drop trees and chocolate pebbles on the beach.

Can you find all the things Tom spotted? How many pebbles can you count?

Chocolate Island

Captain Cook handed Grace a small purse when they landed. "These are Chocolate Island pennies," she said. "Watch out for the sinking syrup and galoptious gloop! And never believe anything the whistling candy trees tell you."

Grace and Tom wondered what kind of place the island was . . . They were about to find out.

Hello! I'm a Chocolate Island guide. Try some rainbow drops, they're tasty.

They saw chocolate everywhere — milk chocolate apples, white chocolate peaches and dark chocolate chestnuts, growing next to real fruit and nuts.

This is Hansel and Gretel's house. They get a bit cross when too many people start nibbling pieces.

"I have to go now," said the guide. "Tiggy will help you find the chocolate well. He's under the tutti frutti tree with chocolate pears and white flowers growing on it."

Can you see Tiggy beneath the tutti frutti tree?

The Chocolate Chip Mine

Lying beneath the tree was Tiggy, a sleepy-looking tiger.

"You're looking for the chocolate well?" he yawned. "Visit the chocolate chip mine first. It's the only one of its kind. You can't visit the island and not see it."

A talking tiger! It was hard to believe. He led them to a small red cable car at the top of the mine shaft.

"I must finish my snooze now," said Tiggy. "After the mine, you should go to the waterfalls."

The cable car rushed down and down. PLING! A bell rang as they hit the bottom. They were in a lofty, brightly lit cavern. On all sides miners were chipping away at the chocolate chunks in the rock. The chips were whisked away to be baked into cookies. Grace wondered how many miners there were.

How many chocolate miners can you see?

Chocolate Falls

When they clambered out of the cable car, Tom and Grace saw the waterfalls ahead. But these were no ordinary falls.

"They look like chocolate milkshake," exclaimed Grace, as she watched the foaming, bubbling liquid tumbling over the rocks.

Tom scrambled down to the rainbow tinted pool at the bottom. "I'm going for a swim," he called, jumping in.

Soon, Grace and Tom were splashing, leaping and diving. As Grace came up for air, she found herself staring into the unblinking eyes of the largest toad she had ever seen. The toad stopped munching chocolate beans and began croaking, loudly. It seemed impossible, but it was giving them a message.

What is the toad's message?

Inside the Cookie Café

"This place is bound to be crammed with scrumptious things to eat," said Tom, at the door to the Cookie Café. He wasn't disappointed. He licked his lips at all the amazing goodies. When the other customers heard the children's quest to find the well, they tried to help.

Just as they were about to leave, Grace noticed something. "Remember Granny Truffle? I've just spotted something that Uncle Ollie would find very useful. Luckily I still have those Chocolate Island pennies we were given."

Can you see what Grace has spotted?

The signpost will point you to the Toffee Tower.

The chocolate well is in the middle of a tricky maze.

Climb the Tower to find your way through the maze to the chocolate well.

Chunky Chocolate Signpost

Outside the café, Grace and Tom turned left along the crispy crackle path. "It's made from chocolate crispies," exclaimed Grace, breaking off a small piece to eat. It was sweet and crunchy.

But Tom was too busy staring at the stream. It was easy to see why it was called the Bubbling Brook. It kept bubbling up into huge balloons which popped loudly. Soon they turned a corner and saw the chunky chocolate signpost to the Toffee Tower in front of them.

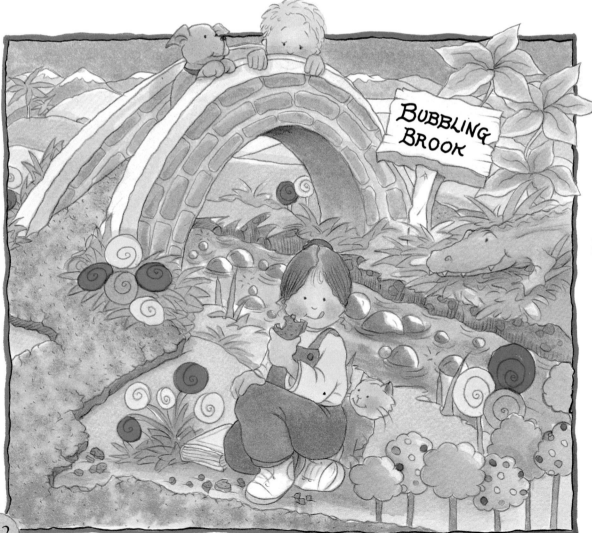

A plump squirrel was perched on top of the post munching. The sign pointed to three paths, but all three pointers had pieces missing. Tom could see the word Toffee on two of them.

He picked up the piece which said Tower. "I know what to do," he said. We just have to match this piece to one of the pointers. Then we'll know which path to take to the Toffee Tower."

Can you match the broken piece to the sign?

Sinking Syrup

As Tom and Grace started along the path to the Toffee Tower, the trees grew thicker and thicker. Soon it was very dark. Tom hurried ahead. Squelch, squelch, schloop! He seemed to be wading through sticky syrup. Suddenly he was sinking – to his ankles, to his knees, then to his waist. "Help!" he yelled.

A very strange thing happened next. The red and white striped candy trees growing on all sides began to whistle and speak!

"Keep going," they whistled. "Wade to the middle, keep to the golden gloop stones and avoid the mossy green ones." Tom was about to follow their advice when Grace stopped him.

"Wait!" she shouted. "Remember what Captain Cook told us when we first arrived? I know what you have to do."

What did Captain Cook say? What do you think Tom should do?

Mallow Maze

Tom still felt sticky when they arrived at the Toffee Tower. In front of it wound the Mallow Maze and in the middle of that was the chocolate well.

"I'll race you to the top of the Tower," called Tom. "From there we can plot our route through the maze to the chocolate well."

They huffed and puffed their way up to a balcony and looked down.

Can you find a way through the maze to the chocolate well?

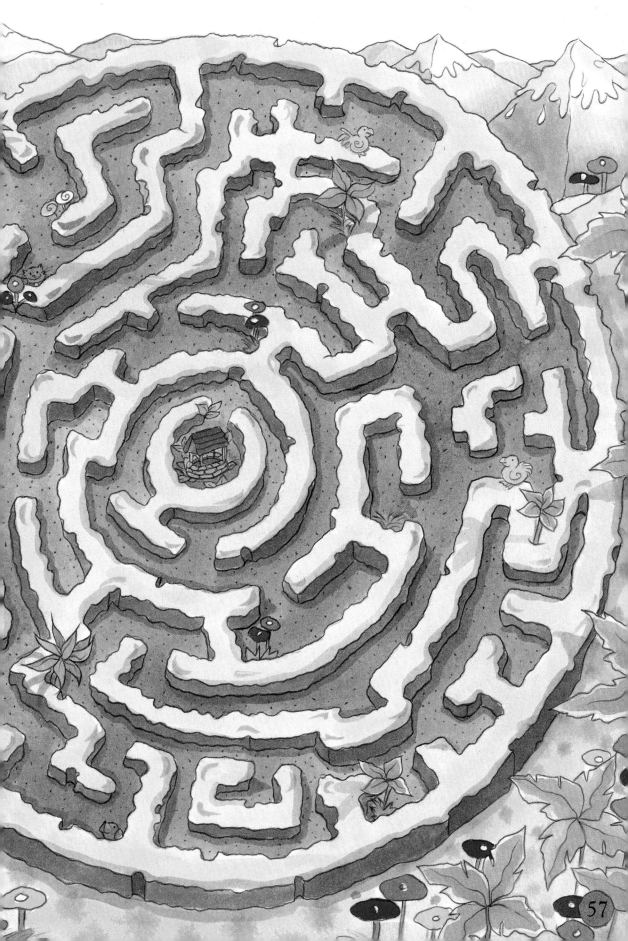

The Chocolate Well

"We're here at last," exclaimed Grace, when they reached the well. "I can't wait to try the chocolate."

Together they hauled up the bucket. There was silence as they licked their lips. It really was THE most delicious chocolate they had ever, ever tasted.

But time was running out. They had to get home quickly if Uncle Ollie was to bake his chocolate cake in time for the competition.

They raced back through the maze, past bubbling streams and waterfalls and all the other amazing sights, back to the beach. But how were they to get home? The ferry was nowhere to be seen. Luckily help was on hand.

What is the time? Is it safe for Grace and Tom to cross the underwater path?

There is an underwater path back to the mainland. It's safe to cross when the water is less than knee deep at low tide.

If there is no ferry you may be able to cross by the underwater path
The water is over your head depth at 8 o'clock
It's shoulder deep at 10 o'clock
Knee deep at 12 o'clock
Ankle deep at 2 o'clock
Toe deep at 4 o'clock

The Competition

Grace and Tom splashed over the watery path, raced across the shore and panted their way back to Uncle Ollie's house.

There was no time to lose. Uncle Ollie happily set to work with scales, pans, mixing bowls, flour, eggs and all the other ingredients that went into Granny Truffle's sensational chocolate cake recipe. Not forgetting the most important of all – the Chocolate Island chocolate.

The finished cake looked perfect and smelled delicious. At the Chunkies Chocolate Cake Baking Competition, the judges seemed impressed. Tom nudged Grace as one after the other, the judges came back for second helpings. There WAS someone who did not look too happy at the way the competition was going.

Can you see who it is? Which one do you think is Uncle Ollie's cake?

Prize Giving

There was silence in the hall. The big moment had come. Mr. Chunky, the chief judge, stepped onto the platform.

"Today, there was one chocolate cake beyond compare, one cake which everyone loved," he said. "The winner is . . . Uncle Ollie."

Everyone cheered and clapped. Smiling happily, Uncle Ollie walked up to receive his prize winner's cup with Grace and Tom. He held it high and gave the toast: "To Granny Truffle and Chocolate Island!"

"And the best ever adventure!" added Tom.

Answers

Pages 36-37
Uncle Ollie's spectacles are here.

Pages 38-39
The map is circled here. You can see the moon and star sign in the corner.

Pages 40-41
Chocolate Island is here.

You can see the Chocolate Island symbol of the moon and star on the signpost.

Pages 42-43
This is Chocolate Island.

You can see the chocolate fudge stream and chocolate drop trees marked here. There are twelve chocolate pebbles on the beach.

Pages 44-45
You can see Tiggy here under the tutti frutti tree.

Pages 46-47
There are eleven chocolate chip miners. You can see them all circled here.

Pages 48-49
The message is:

GO TO THE
COOKIE CAFÉ

Pages 50-51

Grace has spotted a sign for Granny Truffles's Chocolate Recipe Book. They can use the Chocolate Island pennies that Captain Cook gave them to buy a copy.

Pages 52-53

The broken piece which says Tower matches this pointer. Grace and Tom must take this path to the Toffee Tower.

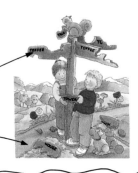

Pages 54-55

Captain Cook told them to: "Watch out for the sinking syrup and galoptious gloop. And never believe anything the whistling candy trees tell you." (See page 44.) Grace knows that Tom should not do what the trees are telling him. To cross the syrup he must only walk on the green stones and avoid the gloop stones.

Pages 56-57

The route through the maze is marked here in red.

Pages 58-59

The clock on the Toffee Tower shows the time is 2:30 and the signpost tells them the water is less than ankle deep at that time.

This means it is safe for Grace and Tom to cross the causeway back to the mainland and home.

Pages 60-61

Mrs. Nougat is not very happy. You can recognize her from page 38. Ollie's cake has the Chocolate Island moon and star sign as decoration.

Mrs. Nougat

Ollie's cake

By the way . . . did you spot Captain Cook appearing throughout the story? You can see her on page 36 at the shop window; on pages 42 and 44 with her boat; helping Tom and Grace on page 59; and as one of the judges on page 61.

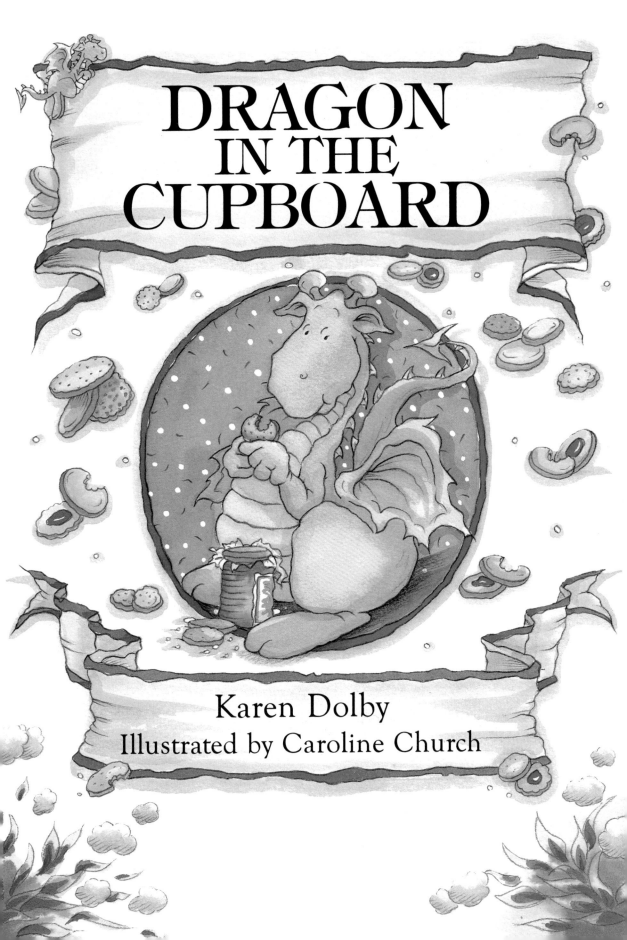

DRAGON IN THE CUPBOARD

Karen Dolby

Illustrated by Caroline Church

Contents

About this Book

Here are George and Lottie. With tummies rumbling, they have gone to the kitchen in search of a small snack. But today everything is not quite as normal. . .

Inside the Cupboard

"Crunch . . . Crackle . . . Munch . . . Slurp . . ." The sounds were coming from a large cupboard in the farthest, darkest corner of the kitchen. Whatever could be inside?

George listened at the door and opened it quietly, just enough to peep inside. GULP! George slammed the door shut. He couldn't quite believe his eyes.

"What is it?" asked Lottie.

Trying to look bold, George grasped the handle and this time flung open the door. There, smiling shyly, its cheeks crammed with food was . . .

"A dragon!" gasped George.

The little dragon nodded and said, "I'm very hungry and . . . and . . . I'm lost." With that, a big tear welled up and began to trickle slowly down the creature's face.

"Please don't cry, we'll help you," said George, while Lottie patted the dragon's paw. "What happened to you?"

"Everything's mixed up and I've got a bump on my head." He gave a loud sniff and began to tell his sad tale.

The dragon's story is mixed up. Can you find out what happened to him?

What's My Name?

"The bump on your head has made you lose your
memory," exclaimed Lottie. "Now we know what
happened to you, we'll soon get you home," she paused.
"You DO know where your home is, don't you?"

The dragon was so upset, he couldn't speak. Finally he
sobbed, "No!"

Trying to cheer the dragon up and take his mind off his
problems, Lottie said, "This is George and I'm Lottie.
What's your name?"

The dragon wrinkled his brow. "It's . . . oh dear, I've
forgotten. I know I had a badge with my name on it, but
now I seem to have lost that too."

"Perhaps you dropped it," suggested George. "Let's look."
Can you spot the dragon's badge? What is his name?

Breathing Fire

Dan the dragon, was very pleased to know his name again. "And you'll be my friends and help me get home?" he asked. George and Lottie nodded. Dan was so excited at this that suddenly . . . WHOOSH!

Flames shot out from the little dragon's mouth. George and Lottie leaped back in surprise as the kitchen filled with clouds of grey smoke.

"Whoops," gulped Dan. "I'm sorry. I forgot myself."

Lottie sniffed. There was a suspicious burning smell. Something had been caught in the flames.

Can you see what has happened?

Granny's Secret

George took Dan's scaly paw. "Come on. Let's get you out of here before you do any real damage. We'll go to Granny's. She'll know what to do." They didn't have far to go as Granny Wendy lived next door.

The door opened before they could knock. "Hello Dan," said Granny Wendy. "I knew you were all on your way."

Dan was puzzled. How did she know they were coming? And how did she know his name? He'd only just found it out himself. But Dan was about to discover that Granny Wendy was no ordinary Grandma. She had an unusual secret.

Do YOU know what Granny's secret is?

The Ancient Book of Maps

Granny Wendy listened carefully to Dan's sad story and then led them to her special magic workroom. Standing on tiptoe she lifted down an old book of maps from the top shelf.

"Phoo!" she blew away the dust. "Atishoo!" the dust tickled her nose.

Granny began turning the crinkled pages. "This is the map of the Wild Westlands. Dragonland is somewhere here."

Can you find Dragonland?

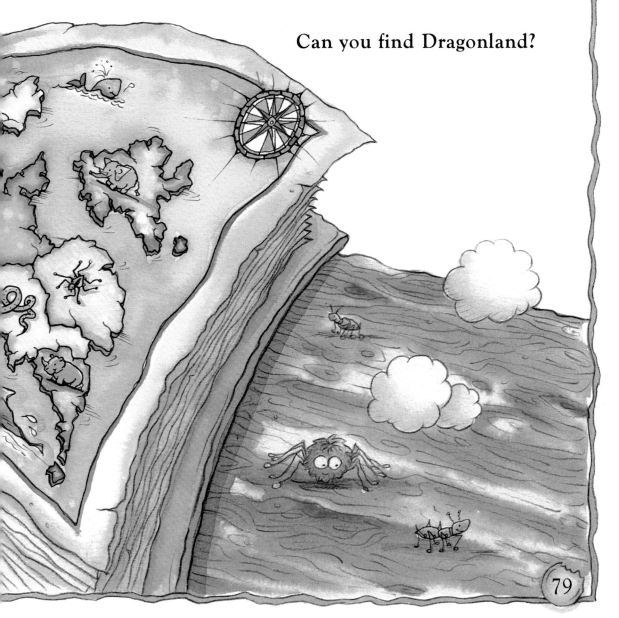

79

The Missing Ointment

"Where exactly do you live in Dragonland?" asked Granny. Dan looked glum. He couldn't think and his bump hurt. But Lottie had an idea. "Granny, why don't you put some of your super-duper magic yellow ointment on Dan's bump. It made my bumped knee much better last week."

Granny Wendy looked surprised. "Did it really? Well I never! I must be getting better at making lotions and potions. There's just one small problem. I don't know where it is. It's in a blue bottle with a black witch's hat on the label."
Can you find Granny's magic ointment?

Granny Casts a Spell

As soon as Granny rubbed the sticky yellow ointment onto his head, Dan began to look and feel better.

"I'm beginning to remember!" he squeaked, excitedly. "The place I live in is called . . . ELLIVNOGARD. "No . . . that's not exactly right. I'm afraid I'm still a bit mixed up."

George thought hard. "The word's not mixed up it's back to front. I know where you live."

Do you?

Meanwhile, Granny Wendy was so encouraged by the success of her yellow ointment, that she decided to try a little more magic to help them on their way to Dragonland.

She checked the list of ingredients in her spell book. "Just a last little pinch of stardust," Granny said, smiling. "And, hey . . ." BANG!

Cave Maze

Spluttering and coughing, Dan, George, Lottie and Granny waited for the smoke to clear.

"Is this Dan's home?" asked George.

"Not quite, dear," said Granny. "Things haven't gone exactly as I planned."

"Can't you magic us out of here?" asked Lottie.

Granny looked worried. She was only halfway through the classes in her "Learn to be a Witch" course. George looked at the paths leading out of the cave.

"We don't need magic," he said. "There is one safe path out to the open air."

Which path will take them safely out of the cave?

Granny Tries Again

Back in the open, Dan's tummy rumbled loudly. He was beginning to wish he had stayed in the cupboard, at least it was full of yummy things to eat. He lay down to dream.

George and Lottie played hide-and-seek. All around they heard the sounds of birds singing and chirping. Bright, exotic butterflies flitted among the trees and flowers. In the distance, the towers and turrets of wonderful castles and palaces glinted in the sun.

Granny Wendy fumbled through her spell book.
"I've found the right spell," she said at last. "I think . . .
But I need one special flower to make it work. It has red,
bell-shaped flowers and green, diamond-shaped leaves
with yellow spots. Can you help me find it?"
George, the dragon and Lottie began the hunt.

Can you find the flower that Granny Wendy needs?

A Fantastic Flight

Clutching the flower, Granny muttered the
magic words. Silence. Nothing happened,
then suddenly: POW! FIZZZ!
Through a purple mist they saw . . .

A unicorn! It seemed to be offering them a ride. It was a tight fit, but somehow they all climbed onto his back and the creature soared into the air. The unicorn left them on a rocky crag. But something was very wrong.

This was NOT Dragonland. Lottie gulped in horror as she spotted a very fierce looking beast.

What has Lottie spotted? What country has the unicorn taken them to by mistake?

Ferocious Beasts

There was no time for another of Granny's spells. There was nowhere to hide and only one way to escape – down the other side of the mountain.

Lottie spotted a boat and Granny thought they could row to Dragonland in it. But first they had to find a safe path down the rocky cliff.

Can you find a safe path down to the boat?

Party Picnic

Safe at the water's edge, Granny nimbly jumped aboard the boat. But just then, a wind sprang up. They heard wings beating the air. A tongue of flame shot past, singeing the grass. With a thud, a small dragon landed in front of them.

"We've been looking for you everywhere, Dan," the dragon exclaimed.

"It's Bess, my sister," whooped Dan.

Bess flew ahead to tell everyone that Dan was not lost anymore and by the time they arrived at Dragonville, a surprise was waiting.

A huge picnic was spread out on the grass and all Dan's family and friends were there.

"It's easy to spot my family," said Dan. "There's Ma, Pa, my sisters Bess and Izzy and brother Arthur. We all have yellow tummies and a green arrow tip at the ends of our tails."

Can you find all the dragons in Dan's family?

Home Again

Dusk was falling and the sun was setting. Even Dan's tummy was full. It was time for Granny Wendy, George and Lottie to go. Dan's Dad offered them a ride home and Dan said he would come along too. They waved goodbye to all their dragon friends and for the second time that day they soared up into the air. All too quickly, they spotted their own house below.

"But I'll see you again soon," smiled Dan. "When you hear strange noises coming from your cupboard you'll know that it's me! But next time, I'll be able to find my own way home."

Answers

Pages 70-71

This is the little dragon's story in the right order:

We went for a picnic. It became very windy. I hit a tree . . .
. . . and fell to the ground. I was dizzy and lost. I saw an open door . . .
. . . and found something to eat.

Pages 72-73

The dragon's badge is here. His name is Dan.

Pages 74-75

Dan's fiery breath has toasted the bread, boiled the milk in the mug, and singed the papers and box of cereal. They are circled below.

Pages 76-77

Granny's secret is that she is a witch. The telltale signs are: the witch's hat, the broomstick and the spellbook, as well as the strange mix of animals in her house.

Pages 78-79

This is Dragonland.

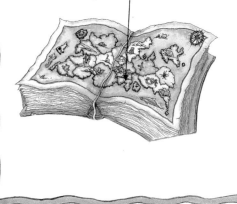

Pages 80-81

Granny's magic ointment is here.

Pages 82-83
The place where
Dan lives is called
DRAGONVILLE.

Pages 84-85
The safe route out of the cave is marked here.

Pages 86-87
Here is the flower that Granny needs.

Pages 88-89
Lottie has spotted a dinosaur.
The unicorn has taken them
to Dinosaurland by mistake.

Pages 90-91
The safe path down to the
boat is marked here.

Pages 92-93
The dragons in Dan's family
are ringed here.

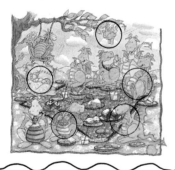

First published in 1995 by Usborne Publishing Ltd,
Usborne House, 83-85 Saffron Hill, London EC1N
8RT, England.
Copyright © 1995 Usborne Publishing Ltd.
The name Usborne and the device 🎈 are Trade
Marks of Usborne Publishing Ltd.
Printed in Portugal
First published in America August 1995.   UE